Mindful Mantras:

I Can Handle it!

Written by **Laurie Wright**
Illustrated by **Ana Santos**

Dedicated to my past students who inspired me to find a way to help, to the 62 generous backers who helped fund the illustrations, to my amazing mojo mamas, and especially to my wonderfully patient husband and children, I love you very much!

Laurie Wright

First paperback edition September 2016

Book design by Ana Santos

ISBN 978-0-995 247 20-8
www.lauriewrightauthor.com

My name is Sebastien,
and I can handle anything!

I'm sad when my best friend is mad at me.
I can handle it though.

I can give him a hug.

I can try to make him laugh.

I can draw a picture!

I can handle it.

I'm frustrated when adults don't listen.
Can I handle it?

I can say, "Excuse me".

I can
write a letter.

I can tell
someone else.

I can handle it.

I'm **mad** when my sister won't stop bugging me.
But I think **I** can handle it.

I can ask her to stop.

I can move away
from her.

I can make it
a joke and laugh.

I can handle it.

I'm annoyed when I can't find my shoe.
Can I handle it?

I can send out
a search party.

I can take out an
ad in the paper.

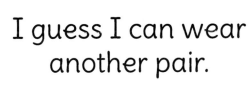

I guess I can wear
another pair.

I can handle it.

I'm disappointed when I want a pet, but I'm not allowed to have one. I can handle this one, I think.

I can pretend
my sister is a pet!

I can make one.

I can play with my
friend's pet in
exchange for him
playing with my sister!

I can handle it.

I feel ashamed when I do something wrong.
Can I handle it?

I can draw an "I'm sorry" picture.

I can do chores without being asked even once!

I can go to my room and stay there until I'm 80!!

I can handle it.

I'm upset when the pool is closed.
But I can handle it.

I can find a
giant puddle to swim in.

I can swim in the tub.

I can save up money
to buy my own pool!

I can handle it.

I feel discouraged when my words don't come out right. But can I handle it?

I can ask a friend
to help me.

I can draw a picture
instead of explaining.

I can sleep on it and
come up with the right
thing to say.

I can handle it.

I'm cranky when I'm not allowed to watch TV.
I can handle it, though.

I can make my own TV
and watch that!

I can act out
my favourite TV show.

I can put on
a puppet show
for others to watch.

I can handle it.

I feel **bored** when I'm stuck at home.
I'm not sure how to **handle** it.

I can make
new slime recipes.

I can build
the best fort EVER!

I can video call
my friends.

I can handle it!

I'm MISERABLE when it's bedtime.
How do I handle that?

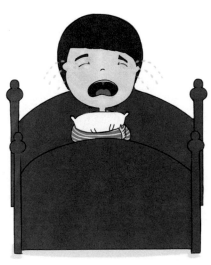

I guess I can cry
myself to sleep.

I can lie in bed
and think about all the things
I get to do tomorrow!

I can count
hedgehogs.

I can handle it.

Sometimes I feel sad, frustrated, mad, annoyed, disappointed, ashamed, upset, discouraged, cranky, bored or miserable.

But I can handle it. I can handle ANYTHING!!

My name is _____

...and I Can Handle ANYTHING!!!

Dear Reader,

I hope that you enjoyed reading about all the different ways you can handle tricky situations! Some ideas were pretty silly, but I think it's fun to be silly sometimes, and I hope you do too.

Next time you feel upset and you aren't sure about how to handle something, stop and think of a few silly things you could do, and then think of a not-silly thing you could do. I know you'll come up with terrific solutions.

If you liked this story and want to read more that are like it, there is a whole series of Mindful Mantra books! They are all on Amazon, waiting for you.

You also might like a song to listen to that helps you remember that you can handle things. Ask an adult to sign up at www.lauriewrighter.com/one if you do.

Finally, a great big THANK YOU for reading, I sincerely hope this book has helped you understand that you CAN handle anything!

All my best,
Laurie Wright

Laurie Wright

Laurie Wright is a speaker, author, and educator who is passionate about helping children increase their positive self-talk and improve their mental health. Laurie speaks to parents, teachers, and childcare providers, has given a TEDx talk, created resources and has written 8 books, all to further the cause of improving the self--esteem of our children. Laurie is a huge advocate for children's mental health and works every day to improve the way we interact with kids, and to help them learn to handle all of their emotions!

Ana Santos

Ana is a creative and innate illustrator and she feels very comfortable and inspired by all the challenges and areas that incorporate illustration and design. Graduated in graphic design, she dicovered her vocation for Arts as a child. Ana has already several years of experience in graphic design and illustration and she has already illustrated several edited children's books for people and publishers around the world! Ana is an artist attentive to new technologies working on many internet platforms as a freelancer.

Made in the USA
Middletown, DE
02 March 2021